If you are not a Men in Black agent,
forget you ever read this.

Go home, turn on the TV, and make a nice dinner.

DO NOT—WE REPEAT—<u>DO NOT</u> TURN THIS PAGE!


THANK YOU.

COLUMBIA PICTURES PRESENTS AN AMBLIN ENTERTAINMENT PRODUCTION IN ASSOCIATION WITH MacDONALD/PARKES PRODUCTIONS A BARRY SONNENFELD FILM
STARRING: TOMMY LEE JONES  WILL SMITH "MEN IN BLACK"™ 2" LARA FLYNN BOYLE  JOHNNY KNOXVILLE  ROSARIO DAWSON  TONY SHALHOUB AND RIP TORN
SPECIAL ANIMATION AND VISUAL EFFECTS BY INDUSTRIAL LIGHT & MAGIC  MUSIC BY DANNY ELFMAN  EXECUTIVE PRODUCER STEVEN SPIELBERG  BASED ON THE MALIBU COMIC BY LOWELL CUNNINGHAM  STORY BY ROBERT GORDON
AMBLIN ENTERTAINMENT  SCREENPLAY BY ROBERT GORDON AND BARRY FANARO  PRODUCED BY WALTER F. PARKES AND LAURIE MacDONALD  DIRECTED BY BARRY SONNENFELD  COLUMBIA PICTURES
MenInBlack.com

Library of Congress catalog card number: 2001094334
Book design by Michael Massen
1  2  3  4  5  6  7  8  9  10
❖
First Edition
www.harperchildrens.com

# MEN IN BLACK II

# THE ALIEN HANDBOOK

## A RESOURCE GUIDE
## FOR MEN IN BLACK FIELD AGENTS

*Written by Agent Zed*
*with help from Michael Teitelbaum*
*Photography by Melinda Sue Gordon*

HarperFestival®
*A Division of HarperCollinsPublishers*

**Terran date:** July 4, 2002
**Universal date:** ⟡◇⟿⚡☌⟊◉⟿✳
**From:** Zed
**To:** All agents of Men in Black
**Re:** Latest alien intelligence reports

First things first: This book does not exist.

If you are a duly authorized Men in Black agent, you know exactly what I mean by that, because, of course, *you* don't exist either. If you are NOT a duly authorized agent of the Men in Black, stop reading now. I don't know how you got your hands on this memo, but someone is going to be in my office tomorrow at 9 A.M. sharp with some explaining to do! Put this memo down and leave the area. In fact, leave the country if possible.

OK, for the rest of you, here's the scoop: A top secret team of our finest agents has been compiling intelligence on the various alien species we have encountered. This handbook is the result of those efforts. The information contained in the following pages will assist you in your sworn duty to protect the Earth from the scum of the universe.

This handbook begins with fact sheets about known aliens—their vital statistics, special abilities, and danger levels. Read this carefully. It could mean the difference between life and death—yours or the entire universe's. I also have included an Alien Assessment Quiz to determine whether or not someone is an alien, as well as a list of helpful alien phrases. Again, this knowledge is critical to your continued success in the Men in Black, not to mention your continued success in breathing.

Read this book, memorize the information within, and then destroy it in the usual manner. (Note to Agent Jay: Blasting it with a Series Four De-Atomizer is not the usual manner, and in fact, falls under the heading of overkill.)

Good luck, study well, and be sure to chew each page thoroughly before swallowing.

Officially yours,

*Zed*

Agent Zed

## Serleena Xath

| | |
|---|---|
| **Home Planet:** | JORN |
| **Height:** | IN HER KYLOTHIAN FORM—12" |
| | IN HER HUMAN FORM — 5' 10" |
| **Age:** | IT JUST WOULDN'T BE HEALTHY TO ASK |
| **Strength:** | EXTREMELY STRONG |
| **Speed:** | MEDIUM |

**Reason for Being on Earth:** To retrieve the Light of Zartha

**Quote:** "My only regret in getting the Light of Zartha off Earth is that it will save this pathetic planet from destruction."

**Likes:** Getting her way

**Dislikes:** Getting bad news

**Special Abilities:** She can ensnare an entire roomful of Men in Black agents in a web-like network of neural roots. This will definitely wrinkle your suit and ruin your day!

**Ambition:** To destroy the planet Zartha

**Weakness:** Dependence on ignorant underlings

**Danger Level:** Extreme

**WHAT YOU NEED TO KNOW:** Born on the planet Jorn in the Kyloth system, Serleena Xath was raised on the planet Kylothia. Kylothia is a planet of warriors whose main goal is to conquer other worlds—particularly the planet Zartha, its nearest neighbor, with whom it has been engaged in a long and costly war for many decades.

In her true Kylothian form, Serleena Xath is a twelve-inch-

long neural root, comprised of nerve tissue, muscle tissue, and tendons. In this form, she slithers like a snake and moves very quickly. But she rarely shows her true form for long.

Ruthless and cunning, once Serleena is on Earth she changes her appearance radically. Her neural tissue has the ability to morph into human-looking skin. She has been known to assume the guise of a beautiful female Homo sapien.

Even in her human form, Serleena can extend deadly neural roots, which may be used to grab an opponent by the throat and lift it off its feet. She can also take on multiple opponents, unleashing a thick web of neural roots. Note: When angry, Serleena has difficulty maintaining her human form, and her neural roots reveal themselves.

Serleena operates as an agent of the Kylothian military.

She has searched the galaxy for years looking for the Light of Zartha—a power source that could save the inhabitants of Zartha if returned to that planet, or be used to destroy them if the Kylothians get ahold of it.

Serleena first came to Earth twenty-five years ago to capture the Light of Zartha, but agent Kay foiled her plans. Since that time, believing that the Light had left Earth, Serleena employed a network of spies to assist in her continued search. She recently returned to Earth, convinced that the Light is still here.

She is not a happy camper.

EXERCISE MAXIMUM CAUTION IF YOU ENCOUNTER THIS ALIEN!

| Home Planet: | BI-CRANIA |
| --- | --- |
| Height: | 6' 0" |
| Age: | 28 EARTH YEARS |
| | (56 BI-CRANIAL YEARS) |
| Strength: | WEAK |
| Speed: | SLOW |

**Reason for Being on Earth:** To gather information on the Light of Zartha; sent by Serleena

**Quote:** "If we go to get the Light of Zartha now, we're gonna miss *Friends*!"

**Likes:** TV, movies, VCRs, *People* magazine

**Dislikes:** The mission for which they were sent to Earth; Serleena

**Special Abilities:** Second head (Charlie) can extend from a backpack on an extremely long neck

**Allergies:** Allergic to Serleena's neural roots, especially when wrapped around their throats

**Ambition:** To watch a movie on DVD, listen to a CD, read a magazine, eat a bag of chips, and take a nap—all at the same time

**Weakness:** Too nice to be a really scary, evil alien—which is their job

**Danger Level:** Minimal, unless pushed by Serleena to do her bidding

**WHAT YOU NEED TO KNOW:** Scrad is a two-headed

being known as a Bi-Cranial. His second head, which lives in a backpack on his back, is named Charlie. Curious and outgoing, Charlie can't resist sticking his rather long neck out, commenting on Scrad's behavior, or poking around where he shouldn't.

Bi-Cranials are basically a benign race, preferring to keep to themselves, occupying their time by pursuing their planet's wide array of leisure activities, such as: humming in two-part harmony and having staring contests with themselves. Needless to say, when Scrad arrived on Earth and saw the numerous forms of entertainment offered on *our* planet, he became an instant pop culture fan.

Scrad was sent to Earth by Serleena to collect information that would lead her to the Light of Zartha. He quickly forgot his mission and became hopelessly addicted to Earth's TV shows, movies, music, magazines, and high-tech toys.

Keep in mind that Scrad's allegiance to Serleena is by no means a sure thing. As with most of her operatives, she holds him through fear and intimidation, not genuine loyalty. This can be used against her if we can convince Scrad that he is safe working with the Men in Black. But stay on guard. Though not purely evil, he is unpredictable, especially when bingeing on reruns of *Gilligan's Island* or *Full House*.

Self-preservation and leisure-time activities are Scrad's highest priorities. We must be sure he feels he is getting both from the Men in Black in order for us to gain his trust. Therefore all agents who may encounter this alien should be equipped with a portable DVD player, computer games, and a *TV Guide* at all times.

## Jack Jeebs

| | |
|---|---|
| **Home Planet:** | NEWHEAD |
| **Height:** | 5' 9" |
| **Weight:** | 180 LBS. |
| **Age:** | 45 |
| **Strength:** | MODERATE |
| **Speed:** | SLOW |

**Reason for Being on Earth:** Profit. Jeebs loves cash. He collects and sells technology and artifacts in his pawnshop.

**Quote:** "I think I have one of those down in the basement."

**Likes:** Money

**Dislikes:** Having his head blown off by a Men in Black agent and having to grow a new one

**Ambition:** To get rich quick. So far, it's not working.

**Special Abilities:** Jeebs has the biological ability to regenerate missing or injured body parts. His head can grow back in approximately thirty seconds.

**Weakness:** He has an annoying personality that rubs Men in Black agents the wrong way

**Danger Level:** Only the equipment he possesses is dangerous. Jeebs himself runs from the first sign of danger.

**Favorite Activity:** Acquiring alien technology—at the right price, of course

**WHAT YOU NEED TO KNOW:** A collector and reseller of intergalactic junk, Jeebs often has just the piece of technology—or information—that an agent needs to crack a case.

# Frank the Pug

| | |
|---|---|
| **Home Planet:** | WUF |
| **Height:** | 1' 3" |
| **Weight:** | 22 LBS. |
| **Age:** | 52 |
| **Strength:** | MODERATE |
| **Speed:** | SLOW |

**Reason for Being on Earth:** To keep an eye on illegal alien activity for the Men in Black

**Quote:** "So I said to Serleena, 'Listen, you pile of squirmy guts, if you don't want me to kick your skinny butt, you'd better come quietly!'"

**Likes:** Working as an agent

**Dislikes:** Being thought of as a real dog

**Special Abilities:** Spying, eavesdropping, gathering information, slobbering

**Ambition:** To be a full-fledged Men in Black agent (preferably Jay's partner)

**Weaknesses:** Hot temper; sometimes confuses chasing UFOs with chasing Frisbees

**Danger Level:** Has a mean bite

**Favorite Outfit:** Jacket, tie, and tail

**WHAT YOU NEED TO KNOW:** Frank the Pug is not a real dog, a fact he will remind you of every chance he gets. Frank came to Earth many years ago. He was one of the first aliens encountered by the Men in Black.

Because of his biological mass and certain physiological restrictions, Frank chose to adopt the physical form of an ugly little pug. (No offense, Frank, since I know you'll be reading this. But come on, you aren't about to win any beauty contests.)

Frank has become a valuable member of the Men in Black team, digging up (sorry, Frank, I couldn't resist) information, tips, and leads for us and keeping his eyes and ears on all illegal alien activity on Earth. Frank's tip was crucial during the Edgar Bug incident, and we've always been able to count on him to pick up the scent (Okay, okay, I'll stop! I promise!) of the darker goings-on among criminal-minded aliens on Earth.

Following Kay's neuralyzation, Frank worked briefly as a field agent, partnering with Agent Jay. In addition to his information-gathering responsibilities, Frank now works as my assistant.

(Not bad for a dog.)

## Stinkor

| Home Planet: | HYDRANT |
| --- | --- |
| Height: | 5' 5" |
| Weight: | 200 LBS. |
| Age: | 29 |
| Strength: | STRONG |
| Speed: | SLOW |

**Reason for Being on Earth:** His terrible smell was so offensive to the inhabitants of his home planet that they told Stinkor to leave.

**Likes:** Eating huge amounts of food in one sitting

**Dislikes:** Baths

**Special Abilities:** Can empty a room in less than ten seconds, simply by walking through the door

**Allergies:** Soap

**Weakness:** His horrible odor can be smelled from a mile away, making it easy for Men in Black agents to find him.

**Danger Level:** Dangerous mostly to the noses of those around him

**Favorite book:** *A Tree Grows in Brooklyn*

**WHAT YOU NEED TO KNOW:** This olfactory-offending alien has been imprisoned at the Men in Black headquarters for the past seven years for various crimes committed against the people of Earth. A breathing mask is suggested for any agent coming in contact with him.

| Home Planet: | ANNELID |
|---|---|
| Height: | 4' 0" |
| Weight: | 80 LBS. |
| Strength: | WEAK |
| Speed: | FAST |

**Reason for Being on Earth:** The so-called Worm Guys arrived on Earth ten years ago to get some coffee for the ruler of their planet. It didn't quite work out that way (see below for details).

**Quote:** "The Men in Black are looking for a few good worms!"

**Likes:** Coffee, TV

**Dislikes:** Being suspended from the Men in Black

**Special Abilities:** Can split in half and become two Geebles, Sleebles, etc.

**Ambition:** To become full-fledged field agents for the Men in Black

**Weaknesses:** Coffee, kleptomania

**Danger Level:** Only dangerous to coffee reserves and office supplies

**Favorite game:** Twister

**WHAT YOU NEED TO KNOW:** The Worm Guys were sent to Earth from their home planet of Annelid. Their mission: to obtain—and return with—some of Earth's most precious

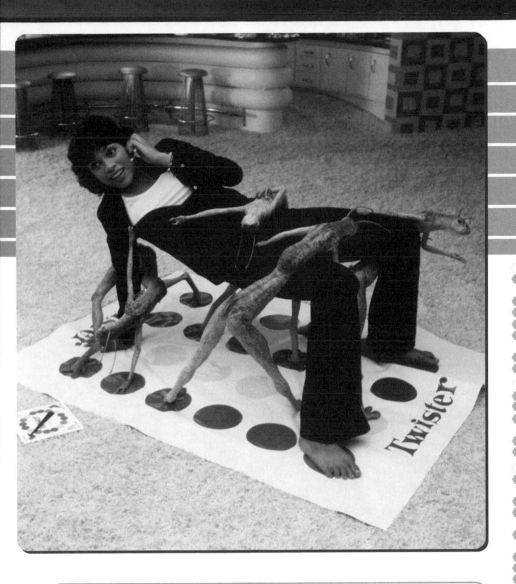

beverage—coffee. The ruler of Annelid was obsessed with finding the finest coffee in the galaxy, and he had heard that much of it was brewed right here on Earth. On Annelid, only the ruler is allowed to drink coffee, so the Worm Guys had never actually tasted the delightful concoction.

While on Earth, they tried coffee. After one taste, the Worm Guys vowed never to return to their home planet again. Instead, they would live on Earth and indulge in this newfound treat. When the Men in Black became aware of their presence on Earth and realized that the Annelids would face dire consequences if they returned home—not the least of which was being forbidden to drink coffee—the Worm Guys were offered positions at the Men in Black headquarters.

Skilled accountants, the Worm Guys took over the bookkeeping department, working efficiently for endless hours, as long as the coffee kept percolating. Their long, thin, worm bodies have arms and legs, allowing them greater dexterity than their tiny Earthly cousins.

The Worm Guys are very proud of the fact that when the Men in Black headquarters was taken over by hostile alien forces, they were called upon to assume the role of commandoes. Usually stuck behind desks, Geeble, Sleeble, Neeble, and Mannix were thrilled to grab some high-tech equipment and join Agents Jay and Kay in their attempt to retake the headquarters.

There have been a few moments, however, that the Worm Guys are not particularly proud of—most prominently, the time they were caught stealing office supplies from the Men in Black headquarters. They were temporarily suspended and forced to remain at home in their messy apartment. I think the long hours of watching TV, hanging out in the hot tub, and playing Twister have taught them a valuable lesson.

| | |
|---|---|
| **Home Planet:** | UNKNOWN (DETAILS BELOW) |
| **Zone Restriction:** | LOCKER C-18 |
| **Height:** | TOO SMALL TO MEASURE |
| **Weight:** | WHY BOTHER? |
| **Strength:** | YOU'VE GOT TO BE KIDDING! |
| **Speed:** | EVEN IF THEY COULD MOVE FAST, WHERE WOULD THEY GO? |

**Reason for Being on Earth:** A crash landing on our planet; Agent Kay helped their civilization (details below)

**Quote:** "All hail Kay! All hail Kay!"

**Likes:** Digital watches, video-store membership cards

**Dislikes:** Being out of touch with the Life Giver (also known as Agent Kay)

**Ambition:** To receive more knowledge from the Life Giver

**Weakness:** They are very, very small

**Danger Level:** None

**Favorite Agent:** Kay

**WHAT YOU NEED TO KNOW:** An entire civilization lives inside a locker at Grand Central Terminal in New York City—locker C-18 to be precise.

These tiny aliens resemble Earth's lemurs, except that their huge eyes take up almost half of their round, flat faces. Two small antennae protrude from the tops of their heads. Small, bony ridges run along their arms and legs.

The aliens of locker C-18 crash-landed on Earth about twenty-five years ago. We believe they were fleeing some kind of tyranny on their home planet, but we've never been able to get the details. Agent Kay found their damaged little starship.

Fortunately, due to their size and certain anomalies in the time-space continuum relative to the theory of relativity, the aliens' entire world fit nicely inside the single locker. (Don't ask me to explain it. I'm no scientist, I just run the joint.) Because Kay found a way to enable them to continue their lives in peace and harmony, the Locker Aliens worship him and are fond of all agents they have met.

They call Kay the Life Giver, for he was able to give them back their way of life—and he also provides occasional pieces of candy. Among the items of worship that Kay has given the Locker Aliens are his digital watch—which they turned into a clock tower, various scraps of food, and a video-rental card that has become regarded as a holy text. The robed and bearded Elder of the Locker Aliens gave his people the rules that were written on the video card:

1) BE KIND, REWIND
2) TWO FOR ONE EVERY WEDNESDAY

These helpful teachings can inspire us all.

# I-C

| | |
|---|---|
| Home Planet: | I-I |
| Height: | 6' 2" |
| Weight: | 205 LBS. |
| Age: | 29 |
| Strength: | MODERATE |
| Speed: | SLOW |

**Reason for Being on Earth:** I-C originally came to Earth to visit his brothers I-O (an accountant), I-D (a security guard), I-Q (a college professor), I-V (a doctor), and I-M (a philosopher).

**Quote:** "Seeing is believing."

**Likes:** Cameras

**Dislikes:** Binoculars

**Special Abilities:** I-C's eye has the ability to see in total darkness and in infrared light.

**Weakness:** Pokes in his eye

**Favorite game:** Peekaboo

**WHAT YOU NEED TO KNOW:** I-C has a very clever disguise. He looks like an ordinary human, but when he pulls off his fake skin, he resembles a centipede with a single large eye on the top of his stalk-like body. I-C's current assignment is keeping an eye (well, he's only got one!) on Agent Kay, while disguised as a postal worker in the Truro, Massachusetts, post office.

# Jeff

| | |
|---|---|
| **Home Planet:** | KRYDILLYON |
| **Height:** | VARIES, BASED ON DIET |
| **Weight:** | NOT MEASURABLE USING EARTH TECHNOLOGY |
| **Strength:** | EXTREMELY STRONG |
| **Speed:** | VERY FAST |
| **Zone Restriction:** | CERTAIN TUNNELS WITHIN THE NEW YORK CITY SUBWAY SYSTEM |

**Reason for being on Earth:** He ate all the nonorganic garbage on his home planet

**Quote:** "ROOOAAARRRR!"

**Likes:** Eating

**Dislikes:** Being told he can't leave the New York City subway system—a feeling he shares with many New York City commuters

**Special Abilities:** He can grow tremendously based on how much he eats

**Ambition:** To eat the entire infrastructure of the New York City subway system

**Weaknesses:** Worm tranquilizers, proton detonators

**Danger Level:** Maximum; can cause unimaginable destruction both below and above ground

**Favorite Food:** Whatever is in his mouth at the moment

**WHAT YOU NEED TO KNOW:** The Krydillyon worm known as Jeff has a simple arrangement with the Men in Black. He doesn't travel outside certain designated areas of the New

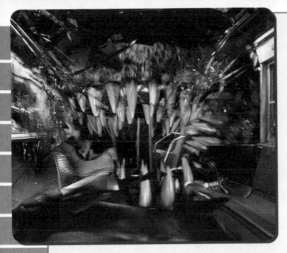

York City subway system, and in return, he can eat all the nonorganic garbage he wants.

Unfortunately, he does not always honor this agreement.

Recently he has violated Men in Black rules, such as: 1) failure to file for movement authorization, 2) appearing unconcealed before the populace at large, 3) attempting to eat subway cars packed with people.

Back on his home planet, Jeff and his fellow Krydillyon worms would have to dig for months, even years, to create an underground home as complex as the many tunnels that make up the New York City subway system. Since his arrival on Earth he has made these tunnels his home, believing that they had been carved out just for him.

Jeff will eat almost anything, and the more he eats, the bigger he grows! Since his skin is resistant to almost all known weapons, you've got a big, strong, hungry alien, who doesn't like being told what to do. His one weak spot is the flower-like stalk on the top of his head, which opens into a small secondary mouth. Men in Black agents have developed a silicon-based serum that when injected into the flower, will put the Krydillyon to sleep. But this serum is not without its problems. It has an extremely short shelf life and must be manufactured constantly in order to be useful.

Let's hope there's enough garbage down in the subway to keep Jeff happy. Usually, that's not a problem.

| Height: | 8' 0" (FLOATING ON DISC) |
|---|---|
| Weight: | 400 LBS. (INCLUDES TITANIUM DISC) |
| Age: | 875 |
| Strength: | VERY STRONG |
| Speed: | EXTREMELY FAST |

**Reason for Being on Earth:** To steal Earth's ozone layer and sell it on the black market to the highest bidder

**Quote:** "I want revenge against Jay!"

**Likes:** Crime for profit

**Dislikes:** Agent Jay

**Ambition:** To acquire wealth by any means possible

**Weakness:** A large supply of flammable fuel in his titanium lower body

**Favorite accomplice:** Serleena

**WHAT YOU NEED TO KNOW:** A master mechanic, he is capable of creating gadgets, weapons, and even vehicles from odds and ends of discarded technology. Jarra's entire lower body has been replaced with an anti-gravity disc made of high-strength titanium, which, of course, he built himself. This flying-saucer shaped disc can move at blinding speeds, making Jarra difficult to catch.

Agent Jay finally arrested Jarra and gathered enough evidence to convict him of stealing part of the Earth's ozone layer and trying to sell it to the highest bidder.

Recently, Serleena freed Jarra from prison. Jarra was reportedly constructing a spaceship for Serleena. This activity must be stopped at all costs, and Jarra must be recaptured. This is a HIGH-PRIORITY ALERT for all active Men in Black agents!

| | |
|---|---|
| **Home Planet:** | HALFLIFE |
| **Height:** | 3' 4" (5' 9" IN HIS HUMAN DISGUISE) |
| **Weight:** | 200 LBS. |
| **Age:** | 36 |
| **Strength:** | WEAK |
| **Speed:** | MEDIUM |

**Reason for Being on Earth:** To escape the hectic hustle and bustle of his homeworld

**Quote:** "Two halves are better than one."

**Likes:** Working at the post office

**Dislikes:** Rude customers

**Weakness:** Sometimes when his human disguise splits in half, Splitz needs help lifting it back onto his small alien body. This occasionally makes it necessary to neuralyze any humans who lend him a hand.

**Zone Restriction:** Truro, Massachusetts

**WHAT YOU NEED TO KNOW:** Splitz stands about three feet tall and walks around on rigid crab-like legs. He has a second set of eyes that grows from the top of his head. This allows him to see through the puppet top half of his human disguise. He is currently assigned to work at the Truro, Massachusetts, post office.

# Lady Bird, Fire Bird

| | |
|---|---|
| Home Planet: | GAMMA |
| Height: | 6' 0" |
| Weight: | 150 LBS. (THAT'S ONE BIG BIRD!) |
| Age: | LADY BIRD, 35; FIRE BIRD, 27 |
| Strength: | WEAK |
| Speed: | FAST |

**Reason for Being on Earth:** The Bird aliens of Gamma took refuge on Earth when their home planet became uninhabitable due to worldwide pollution.

**Quote:** "Nice view from up here."

**Likes:** Wind currents

**Dislikes:** Pollution

**Ambition:** To live safely on Earth in exchange for assisting the Men in Black

**Special Abilities:** They possess superhuman (or in their case, superGamman) sight, and have been great allies to the Men in Black working as guards, spies, and lookouts.

**Weakness:** Sunflower seeds (they can't get enough of them!)

**Favorite song:** "Fly Me to the Moon"

**WHAT YOU NEED TO KNOW:** The Bird aliens of the planet Gamma have found sanctuary on Earth, following the obliteration of their homeworld by pollution. In exchange, they lend their services to the agents of the Men in Black, using their incredibly enhanced vision to work with the agency's operatives.

# Corn Face

| Home Planet: | KERNEL |
|---|---|
| Height: | 6' 4" |
| Weight: | 202 LBS. |
| Age: | 42 |
| Strength: | EXTREME |
| Speed: | SLOW |

**Reason for Being on Earth:** Official reason—to open a roadside farm stand; real reason—to engage in whatever illegal activity comes his way

**Likes:** Fighting with humans

**Dislikes:** Being confined to a Men in Black prison cell

**Ambition:** To get revenge against every agent who has ever arrested him (and there have been quite a few)

**Special Abilities:** Twice the strength of an average human being, and a nasty temper to go along with it

**Weaknesses:** Melted butter, salt

**Danger Level:** Extremely dangerous

**WHAT YOU NEED TO KNOW:** Strong and temperamental, Corn Face is one of the most dangerous foes of the Men in Black. He is a repeat offender who always manages to slip through the legal system on a technicality. NEVER, I repeat, NEVER attempt to detain Corn Face without backup.

# Third-Eye Guy (Teg)

| | |
|---|---|
| **Home Planet:** | SEEWELL |
| **Height:** | 6' 2" |
| **Weight:** | 186 LBS. |
| **Age:** | 76 |
| **Strength:** | VERY POWERFUL |
| **Speed:** | MEDIUM |

**Reason for Being on Earth:** To work as a spy for Serleena

**Quote:** "Serleena, you're a sight for sore eyes—all three of them."

**Likes:** Trifocals

**Dislikes:** Bifocals

**Special Abilities:** An extra or "pineal" eye that rests on the top of Teg's forehead is excellent for secret surveillance missions

**Weakness:** Eyestrain

**Zone Restriction:** New York City limits

**Danger Level:** He is even stronger than he looks. Use caution when dealing with Third-Eye Guy

**WHAT YOU NEED TO KNOW:** Over the years, Teg has been questioning all aliens on Earth in an attempt to gather information about the Light of Zartha. He prefers to keep the eye on his forehead covered with a cap. This makes it easier for him to infiltrate human society.

# Mosh

| | |
|---|---|
| Home Planet: | PLANTATION |
| Height: | 5' 5" |
| Weight: | 245 LBS. |
| Age: | 234 |
| Strength: | STRONG |
| Speed: | MEDIUM |

**Reason for being on Earth:** To get lots of good sunshine in order to produce chlorophyll and bloom

**Quote:** "Can't a talking plant get a break around here?"

**Likes:** Fertilizer

**Dislikes:** People who forget to water their houseplants

**Special Ability:** Photosynthesis

**Weakness:** Fungal infections

**Favorite Snack:** Plant food

**WHAT YOU NEED TO KNOW:** Mosh is an intelligent plant-like creature who produces chlorophyll rather than blood. The thick dangling bulb at the end of his nose contains seeds for perpetuating his race. Mosh is rowdy and always ready for a fight, so Men in Black agents encountering him should be on their guard.

| | |
|---|---|
| **Home Planet:** | TENDRILLIAN |
| **Height:** | 6' 4" |
| **Weight:** | 220 LBS. |
| **Age:** | 76 |
| **Strength:** | MEDIUM |
| **Speed:** | FAST |

**Reason for Being on Earth:** To smuggle unauthorized technology back to his homeworld

**Likes:** Spreading his race's interstellar form of graffiti, which we on Earth call "crop circles."

**Dislikes:** Having to disguise himself by wearing a fake beard. This makes it hard for Gayroon to breathe, which he does through his facial tendrils.

**Special Abilities:** Can filter hydrogen from the air—which he needs to breathe

**Weakness:** He's easy to subdue when you yank on his facial tendrils

**Danger Level:** Gayroon is extremely knowledgeable about all major forms of Earth and alien technology. He also has strong contacts in many major alien underworld crime syndicates.

**WHAT YOU NEED TO KNOW:** Gayroon was once a trusted member of the Men in Black, until it was discovered that he was smuggling unauthorized technology. He is currently in prison where we would like to keep him, since he has contacts in so many alien criminal organizations.

| | |
|---|---|
| **Home Planet:** | KALA-MARI |
| **Height:** | 3' 0" |
| **Weight:** | 80 LBS. |
| **Strength:** | WEAK |
| **Speed:** | SLOW |

**Reason for Being on Earth:** To act as a translator for spoken words or telepathically driven thoughts

**Likes:** Pleasing its owner

**Dislikes:** Its brain-in-a-bubble look

**Special Abilities:** Robot Squid is a biomechanical creation that serves its owner as a translation unit

**Favorite Assignment:** Translating for a high-level inter-galactic political convention

**WHAT YOU NEED TO KNOW:** Sometimes the Robot Squid can do its job too well. It can detect the slightest lie, which it doesn't hesitate to announce. Some space pirates have been known to use the Robot Squid as a lie detector.

## ARE YOU AN ALIEN?
## TAKE THIS QUIZ AND FIND OUT!

Now that you've read and memorized the information in this book about aliens, you are required by Men in Black regulations to take this test to determine whether or not *you* are an alien.

—Zed

1) **You notice that someone wearing a baseball cap is following you. When he takes off his cap to scratch his head, you spot a third eye on his head. Do you:**

   ⓐ Steal his hat with your tentacle

   ⓑ Use your four sets of vocal chords to emit an ear-shattering screech

   ⓒ Tie your legs into a knot to confuse him

   ⓓ Run home and lock the door

2) **A small blob of purple goo asks you for directions. Do you:**

   ⓐ Answer with your second head

   ⓑ Take off in your antigravity belt

   ⓒ Look for a Robot Squid to translate what the blob is saying

   ⓓ Step around the blob so you don't get any goo on your shoe

3) **A beautiful woman asks you if you have seen the Light of Zartha. Do you:**

   ⓐ Answer her instantly and tell her all you know

ⓑ Attempt to withdraw your head into the thick armor that covers your body

ⓒ Turn yourself into a small blob of purple goo

ⓓ Tell her, "No, I haven't seen that movie yet."

**4) A small creature—part spider, part bunny—races past you at top speed. Do you:**

ⓐ Stick out your forty-foot-long tongue and trip it

ⓑ Fire up your titanium lower body and zoom past it

ⓒ Remove your human-looking upper body to get a better look

ⓓ Rub your eyes and decide never to eat twelve pounds of gummy bears in one sitting again

**5) You hear that an alien spaceship has landed in a park near your home. Do you:**

ⓐ Gather your fellow six-foot-tall crickets and see if you can steal anything from the ship

ⓑ Say, "It's about time Breezlop came home. That's the last time I give him the keys to the atomized-turbo-zip-ship!"

ⓒ Pack your bags and prepare to return to your homeworld

ⓓ Race right over with your camera, a lawn chair, and a bag of chips

**6) You're watching an old science fiction movie in which a creature who appears to have no head walks on a set of legs, then flips upside-down and walks on a second set of legs. On the way out of the**

theater you see the same creature do the same thing in the parking lot. Do you:

- a) Ask him for an autograph for your mother back on Hexlathe IV
- b) Challenge him to a gymnastics competition in your zero-G media room
- c) Extend a point from the top of your head, then spin around on it to impress him
- d) Tell him to take off his costume and show you what he really looks like

7) **Some four-foot-tall worms surround you and ask if you've got any coffee. Do you:**

- a) Take them to the nearest diner and buy them each a cup
- b) Tell them to get back to their desks at the Men in Black headquarters at once
- c) Challenge them to a game of Twister
- d) Try to find out what kind of fertilizer was used in the garden in which they lived to make them grow so big, then run out and get some for yourself

8) **You wake up in the morning, look in the mirror, and see tendrils growing from your face. Do you:**

- a) Deliver a shipment of stolen technology to Jeebs' pawnshop
- b) Put on your fake beard
- c) Sneak out the back door to avoid being seen by Men in Black agents
- d) Rush to your dermatologist's office

**9) You look into your locker and see an entire civilization of tiny beings. Do you:**

(a) Give them a gift so they will worship you

(b) Ask to speak to their elder in order to gain wisdom

(c) Close the locker door immediately so that no humans can see them

(d) Realize you haven't washed your gym shorts in a couple of weeks

**10) You go to buy a newspaper from a man at a newsstand. A small pug dog sits beside him. Suddenly the dog begins to speak. Do you:**

(a) Ask the dog for the latest info on illegal alien activities

(b) Start a conversation with the dog in his native language

(c) Extend a neural root and peer directly into the dog's mind

(d) Say, "nice doggie" and congratulate the man on his terrific ventriloquist act

If you answered mostly d, you are probably NOT an alien.

If you answered mostly a, b, or c, you probably ARE an alien and should report to my office at the Men in Black headquarters tomorrow morning at 9 A.M. sharp!

—Zed

Though different alien races speak a variety of languages, this list contains the five most popular phrases that appear across cultures:

**Alien:** 

**English translation:** "Please remove your neural root from my ear."

**Alien:** 

**English translation:** "Which of your heads would like to look at the check?"

**Alien:** 

**English translation:** "You must be wearing contacts. The eye on your forehead is a different color from the other two on your face."

**Alien:** 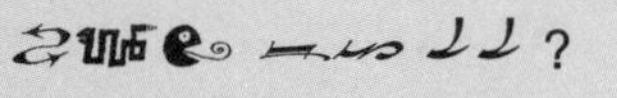

**English translation:** "Does that train you just ate stop at 42nd Street?"

**Alien:** 

**English translation:** "There is just no way you could have made that crop circle on the ground without leaving any tire marks!"

**1** **(To Jarra)** Does that flying saucer take regular or premium?

**2** **(To The Locker C-18 Aliens)** Do you get out much?

**3** **(To Split Guy)** Have you ever put your top half on backward?

**4** **(To Scrad/Charlie)** What do you do if you each want to watch a different movie?

**5** **(To Serleena)** If you do find the Light of Zartha, are you going to put it on an end table in your living room?

*"You know, I may look like a dog, but actually, I only play one here on Earth."*